THE
URGE
WITHIN ME

THE URGE
WITHIN ME

PETER KNOESTER

Kravitz & Sons
INNOVATORS IN PUBLISHING, MARKETING AND ADVERTISING

Kravitz and Sons LLC
204 E Arlington Blvd. Suite B
Greenville, NC 27858

© 2025 Peter Knoester. All rights reserved.

No part of this book may be reproduced, stored in a retrieval system, or transmitted by any means without the written permission of the author.

Published by Kravitz and Sons LLC.
ISBN: 979-8-89639-474-7 (sc)
ISBN: 979-8-89639-473-0 (e)

Library of Congress Control Number: 2026905233

Because of the dynamic nature of the Internet, any web addresses or links contained in this book may have changed since publication and may no longer be valid. The views expressed in this work are solely those of the author and do not necessarily reflect the views of the publisher, and the publisher hereby disclaims any responsibility for them.

Table of Contents

The reason for writing this I hardly understand myself it seems that there is an urge in me to do so just as there is a reason or no reason for the emigration of birds, animals, fish, butterflies and all other living creatures that have an urge to go to better pastures as it were or to mate and reproduce or have babies. Even plants have in them the urge to grow either from a seed or bud or any other means. There is an unstoppable force at work here that we don't really understand some call it Mother Nature although I believe there is much more than that at work here. I believe The Creator has instilled in every growing thing an urge to be more than it is in itself and to expand as it were to something bigger and better than it was when it started. The same urges live in us and make us what we are or will be when the grow stops, if it ever will.

The expression the grass is always greener at the other side becomes a way of life for some of us and so we will never be satisfied with what we have as long as that urge or outlook is there. You may be thinking Where is he going with that and I will get to the point soon enough. All of us have instilled in us the same forces that an animal or plant has and that is to grow and become one with the creator or better put with our Creator. There seem to be so many ways to become one with the Creator that we easily can become lost and to choose the right path is surely not easy. There have been and are so many religions in the world today and depending into which family we are born we follow the path that our parents have set out for us. We have as it were no choice in this especially as young children.

It is only when we get older or become adults that we see the world in a different light. It is so easy to become part of a herd that is pulled in this or that direction by the drovers that we remain on the path of all the others in the herd. The different religions like Islam, Buddhism, Hinduism, Christianity, all have their own way of becoming one with the Creator especially the Christian churches who have been so splintered over the centuries that very little has remained of the teachings by the apostles of old or of Jesus Christ Himself. I realize that I have made quite a jump here by bringing in the Christ figure but I believe that there is no other way to become one with the Creator than getting to know this figure as told to us by the Bible.

I was brought up as a Christian; Heaven knows that I am no saint and strayed so far that the chance to get back was slim-to-none but here I am and I am writing all this down to express myself to others who may be in the same boat. The urges in us were put there by our Creator to give us the chance to become one with Him and to get to know His Son as well as the Holy Spirit from whom this urge comes. In the history of the Hebrew people and their writings in the Torah, from which we have our Old Testament, it has been always the same, a sacrifice had to be made in order to take away the sins committed either by the people or by the individual. It could be a lamb a dove or another pure animal whose blood was spilled to satisfy God's demands for the forgiveness of the sins committed. This was the way it was done by the high priest of the day and was a prelude to the way the sins of all the people in the world who were willing to become one with the Creator would live until all eternity in Heaven.

THE RULER OF THIS WORLD

Yes indeed who is the ruler of this world. Christ mentioned him in the New Testament saying that the ruler of this world did not want anything to do with Him because he knew that He was the one who came into the world to dethrone him and loose the people from his clutches. Let there be no mistaken about this, the ruler of this world is Satan and his cohort. He was in the Garden of Eden in the very beginning and enticed the newly created beings to disobey their Maker and to believe him, the father of all lies. The terrible consequences of his intrusions into the affairs of man cost mankind eternal life and the only way mankind could be saved from eternal condemnation was with the coming of Him Who would be called the Christ and redeemer of mankind who would give them a way to escape as it were the clutches of Satan and his cohorts. To be sure Satan is one of the most intelligent entities in the world; through him we have all the games people play, all the music that was created, and all that was invented and made by him including all that plays on the airwaves to make the people of this earth knowledgeable about the way to eternal life. Most of us don't really understand the reason for this until we reach a certain age and then we become aware that we won't live forever and the dread of eternal damnation comes more and more to the fore. I realize that there are so many different religions in the world today and all claim that their way is the right one to achieve eternal life and people live according to what that sect, religion, or belief tells them and that is what is called freedom of religion as the government cannot impede it unless they become a totalitarian government. For most of us who live in the so-called western world, Christianity is the main religion historically, and with it comes the Bible as we know it, divided into two parts, the Old and the New Testament. It is perhaps mostly of Jewish origin though the New Testament is not a part of the Jewish faith. As such to us in the western world the Bible is the only way to eternal life. I have come to realize that religion and the relationship with our God is of a very personal nature and should be respected by others and not ridiculed or laughed at. Well I had my say and will now close as my thoughts on this are now on paper for everyone to see.

DUST OF THE EARTH

When I am listening to the songs sung by the people that are long gone and see the young faces that once were so beautiful and full of life I am so saddened that a tear starts to flow and my eyes become misted over. I come to see how everything is so temporary and how life no matter how old one gets is but a very small thing compared to the universe and the age of it. We all walk the road that is set out to us and I know we must do the best we can even though that is not always easy. There is such a longing in me to become one with it all and to understand the real meaning of life and the reason for it all. I know that here we understand only partly but when the day comes that it will not only make sense but we will become one with it all and be part of that great adventure if you will and the truths come to the fore that indeed will make us free and like God we will be all-knowing as we will be part of His kingdom and a part of Him who did not spare His only begotten son but gave Him over to those who crucified Him to as it were buy us for the Father. What are we but made of the dust of the earth, still we are mightier than any mountain as we have life in us while a mountain has just rock and stone and is as cold as an iceberg, or can be.

THE PASSING OF TIME

Today is the 23rd of April and I am listening to some beautiful music from some of the great composers of all time. I love to hear them again and again. The thing that saddens me is the fact that they are all gone now and the great voices of the past have also succumbed to the Angel of Death. I am asking myself the question Where are they now Are they with God or are they awaiting judgment along with everybody else, even the great kings of the past Are they all there in the same place. Is there any conversation between them and are they relating to what they were on Earth and all the things they did while there. I know I am being silly perhaps and live in another world that only I know about or think of. To the questions there is no end they keep coming and there is not really an answer only speculation.

WHAT HEAVEN IS LIKE

As I sit here at my computer I am trying to envision what Heaven is like and what it is all about. I have tried to tell about this in one of my other writings but in reality no one knows what Heaven is like. One thing we can be sure of is that that which is unclean will never enter nor be there. We as human beings tend to think earthly things and can hardly understand or comprehend what a spiritual world looks like. I don't believe that an earthly body will reside there. Heaven is a spiritual realm where the spirits of those who were found in Christ are gathered to sing praises to the One who, through his suffering and death, has obtained forgiveness for sins of all the chosen ones. When I was talking to a friend of mine a while back I mentioned to her that there are no computers in Heaven. I have since come to realize that this was something that kind of slipped out of my mouth and I have come to see the consequences of this expression. What is it that those who have the privilege of being in Heaven do all day long, or are there only days. What is it that binds us all together, is it the fact that we were saved through the Son of God and is that the topic of our conversation, or will there be no need to talk because we will be like God: all-knowing. When I am thinking this over I see what an utter fool I am to try to explain the unknown. Christ foretold that in His Father's house are many mansions and if this was not so He would not have told us. Could we look upon this as being an eternal holiday or like a storybook ending when it states "And they lived happily ever after."

WHERE AM I

What unspeakable torment the soul feels even while it is lost in all its familiar surroundings. Wanting to grab a hold of anything that will tell it it is not lost but just bewildered because of an event that was perhaps outside of its control. Friends look at you and nod their heads as if they know what you are going through. When past events overwhelm one with waves of fresh memories, a life long forgotten, but wave after wave reminds one that in the far corner of the mind it still lurks. I know these thoughts are buried under so many other things but like a worm it works its way out of chaos and shows itself at the most inopportune moments. Will we ever be free again or are the events of the past like a guard keeping us prisoner for as long as we live. I realize that not all of us are in this state but most of us are, for who is perfect and without sin. For some the conscience is seared shut as with a hot iron and for those there is no hope of any redemption as they will not even recognize their own deeds for what they are. But for all the others that do experience the pangs of regret and wish to be unburdened there is hope. As you can tell my thoughts and other writings always turn to the religious side as what else is there. I suppose a psychiatrist could be of some help but in the long run the thoughts will return and we are back into the same rut as it were as before. The only way to be rid of all our burdens is through the forgiveness of sins and the only one who can do this for us is Jesus the Christ and Him only.

RELIGION MADE EASY

This of course is a white lie as religion is a way of life for many a person and certain strict rules have to be observed. It is obvious that the reason for religion, whether you are a Christian, Muslim, Buddhist, Hindu or whatever is to obtain eternal life in the hereafter. Personally I am of the Christian faith and to be sure many a book has been written by people with personal experiences as to how they obtained knowledge of eternal life. We of the Christian faith got most of our knowledge about the way to Heaven from the Torah. The Bible of the Christian faith has in it most of the history of the Jewish nation divided into two parts, the "Old" and the "New" testaments. Christians rely on our Bible to be the word of God Almighty and we cannot take anything away from it lest we fall away into chaos. The Old Testament relates to the beginning of mankind after Creation and the subsequent history of mankind, mostly of the Israelites and their travels and all the events that transpired until this day. In the Old Testament we find the prophets of old who foretold events included the coming of a Messiah who would give his life and blood for the cleansing of the sins of anyone who believed in Him and so obtain eternal life. I realize that this is the short version of the way to Heaven, etc. We have to understand that the Trinity, consisting of God the Father, God the Son, and God the Holy Spirit are all involved in this process of the born again experience, which is in short a denial of the self, instead living for Him who gave his life. I know this is a deep subject and has to be understood spiritually where the relationship between the creation (You and I) and the Creator is of the utmost importance. We of ourselves do not see anything beyond the end of our noses but when the Holy Spirit enters into the hearts of men then the light of eternal life will start to shine into our hearts and we, though not fully able to see this, can look, as the apostle Paul says, through a dark glass into what will be ours to claim through the power of the Spirit made available through the Trinity. There are so many books written about this subject by people who have experienced this transformation and to read up on this can give us an additional light upon things pertaining to the eternal.

THE ENDING

Here I am sitting listening to the psalms sang so long ago that pull on my heartstrings. They take me back to the days of my youth and when my sisters and my parents were still living. The tears are running down my cheeks because I feel so forsaken and the memories of yore are still as vivid as when I was there at the time. I am so sorry for it all and the things that have happened to me. I deserve and I know this. The good Lord has visited me and taught me lessons that my heart understands but my brain does not accept. To the whys there is no end and even if I acknowledge everything from a to z it has or wants to find an escape even though the doors are shut and I must absorb the blame whether I like it or not. The thoughts that come to me when this is happening try to say to my heart It is not so bad, even though I know better. There is always this notion that there are people who are so much more evil than I or who have committed awful sins against mankind like Hitler or a godfather of a gang. I know it is all in vain and I realize that we all are responsible for the deeds we have done and have to take whatever is allotted to us in this life. I also realize that even though I could have been condemned to a very lonely life the Lord saw fit to bring somebody into my life who has been my lifesaver and to whom I owe an immeasurable debt. I have come to see that God has been merciful to me, who deserves none if this. Now I am getting older and when I look at the obituary column and see so many people passing on who are my age and younger I know that the end is coming with the speed of a freight train and there is no stopping this train. Thankfully there is an escape route given by the Saviour of all mankind for those chosen to be saved. I am trying to understand it all and have so many books on this subject and have only read so few of them. Now, as I think I am almost there already and ready to go out of this life, even though my soul is crying out to Him who knows my heart and has been with me all my life ,whether I recognized it or not, I am so impatient as to what will become of me in the now as well as in the future.

There is now talk of a pending disaster that will take place later this year as an until now unknown planet will enter into our planetary orbit and will do great damage to the earth, so much so that very few people will survive this catastrophic event. So now we will ask ourselves Will the lives of so many be lost or is there an escape from this terrible event. I don't want to become a preacher but in the Bible we find a way to escape all this via what is called the rapture as those who believe in the redeemer Christ and accept Him as their Lord and the Saviour of their soul. I know this is one of the shortest versions of the reborn experience but I thought to put this on paper nevertheless. I can well imagine the great events that will take place if what is being said about a pole shift will take place as it has taken place before as described by Immanuel Velikovsky in his book Earth in Upheaval. According to Bible prophesies the islands will disappear and the oceans will cover the lowlands and the mountains will be shoved about like so many pebbles and whole plates will slide over the older ones and destroy everything in their path. Volcanoes will erupt and cover large areas and the smoke of it all will cause the sunlight to shine as though through a sackcloth and the moon will not be seen nor the stars and the recovery if any will take so very long that nobody can survive except a very few who have been ready. A lot of people will say What is he talking about and you are right

who am I to tell you about this and I don't even know myself
Why I am putting all this on paper. But here it is my thoughts
about the ending for this world as we know it. May God have
mercy on all the children.

THE CREATION OF THIS WORLD AND ITS PEOPLE

What can be said about this world and its people and to what purpose is it all here. There are so many books written about how we the people got here in the first place. Personally I am in favour of The Big Bang theory in the which all the universes were created. If you believe in a Godlike entity as the Creator or even if you don't there are two main factions that think they have an answer for the why and the how. One is that we came from a single cell that somehow reproduced itself and was able to produce a living thing that went from a small microbe to producing all living things depending as to what this living cell had in mind or was directed by force of nature to accomplish. It first produced an algae of a kind then plants like grass then shrubs then trees and so on and all the flora was made from the start of a single come-to-life cell. The other is the belief in the Creator who is all-powerful and all-knowing and has the ability to make something out of nothing. If the Big Bang was the start of it all then if an entity like that can do this, creating all the universes including our Milky Way in a moment then why would it be so hard to create anything at all and to maintain it until this day. Yes there is the story of creation as told us in the Christian Bible and a lot of people do believe that everything was created in seven days. For myself I don't believe this and it must not be taken literally as one day is by God as a thousand years or even a million years. So if we follow the Bible story about creation it follows that our world must have been a molten mass of rock and all the elements that are found in it to this day and our sun that was created at the same time could not be seen because of the smoke that must have surrounded the world. And it must have taken perhaps a million years before the earth cooled off enough and the smoke cleared so that the sun was able to shine on the earth. There is evidence that during the cooling off period the earth was bombarded with meteors as well as asteroids that must have been made of solid ice and subsequently melted and formed oceans as well as lakes of a sort and produced rain clouds from the steam which caused the earth to cool even more as the power of the sun was thwarted. It is said in the Bible story that God's spirit hovered over the waters and it began to produce all vegetation and trees of all kinds came into being. This must have taken perhaps another million years. By then the stars and the moon could be seen clearly. The life giving spirit now took over as it were and created all the living things that would ever be in the sea or in the oceans or in the air and they too were in their element for say another million years. At the same time there was the creation of all the animals that will ever live on the earth including cattle, etc. It is my belief that the dinosaurs in all their splendour were also on the earth but were not in the plan of the Creator when mankind came into being and so they were done away with through natural disasters or whatever was needed to do away with them. If an entity or Godlike person could create all that we see and know about the universe then how hard would it be to create a man and a woman in His own image and to maintain them until this day. The reason for the creation of mankind I will write about at a later date.

Well the later date is here and I wanted to start by telling you about the creation of man. It states that the "Trinity" (the Father, the Son and the Holy Spirit) decided to make man in their own image to live on this beautiful world now fit for habitation and so did create Adam and Eve and from their descendants all of mankind came into existence. It is also stated in Genesis that the first people were not allowed to eat from a certain tree but in disobedience to their Maker they did so anyway and were now condemned to live outside of Paradise which was where they lived after they were created. Because of their Sin as it was now called all of mankind was condemned to die and although in the beginning they were getting very old, in the end they were mortal. When mankind was created each was given a living soul and it was that part that would live forever even after they died and it is that part of mankind that is the main cause for creation. God knew that all this was going to transpire and had a fail safe plan in mind to replace all the fallen angels by creating man and from them take those who would be found worthy to become an angel in Heaven or take the place of one of them. Now, in one part in the Bible where it states that an angel, later called Beelzebub or Satan as we know him, residing in Heaven, decided that he was as good as the Creator, God, even though he was himself a created being. Satan rebelled against God, so God had to banish him from the heavens and did so. Satan went with one third of the heavenly beings, who followed him to the earth where he resides and rules along with his fellow satanic angels. Here on Earth, Satan and his henchmen are directing almost all of this world's affairs by infesting the minds of many to entice and to tempt them to do all kinds of evil things. There is no way of stopping them we can only be on guard and resist the temptations by living according to the Bible's scriptures. Our all-knowing God has known from the beginning of creation that this would take place and so found a way to make new angels by sending His Son to the earth to be a sacrifice for those willing to accept Him as their saviour and to do all what God commands of all living human beings. This is the only way for our soul to live eternally with God in the heavens.

LOOK, LOOK INSIDE

What do we see an old man who was subjected to so many ways of killing the emotions and the happiness of life that he is now only a shell of what he was if he ever was the way he thought he was. How come he is so dead inside, so much so that he is just living, breathing, eating, and sleeping his life away. So many disappointments have done him in and his behaviour has been questionable to say the least. Man, what happened in his youth How did he become the person that he is. Was it his parents his upbringing and all that they brought with them. The strict rules that had to be adhered to Or was it something he was born with and that manifested itself later on in life. To the questions there is no end and I am sure that during his lifetime many more will come to the fore.

MELODIES OF THE HEART

There is no doubt that within us there is a desire to express ourselves through whatever means and if it were possible through a song that only we know and of which the melody is unknown to anyone but ourselves. I wish in a way that when we met a song was coming out of us and thus was letting the other person know how we feel and what they mean to us. I must add that there could be a lot of embarrassments as well as joys to know what the other person means to us, and then I am glad that this is not so. We can express ourselves to others in so many different ways with words and deeds. So many times I wish I would have expressed myself more deeply to a person who has passed away and it leaves me with an empty feeling that cannot be overcome at times. I know the memories always remain and to do unto others who we have contact with the things that aught to be done is a good thing to do. The word love is at times overused and the real meaning of love is in a way watered down. So many people meet and before you know it they are in love as they say and want to get married right away and than they find that their so-called love was an attraction to each other with no real anchor and the marriage ends up in divorce. The tremendous loneliness caused by these actions can be very devastating to a person. I hope that a real melody of love will live in us and will express itself to others to make the world a better place for many a lonely soul.

MY CRY

O God I am so hopelessly lost in time and the presence of space. The huge boulders of the ages have become an obstacle that I don't seem to be able to overcome. The lessons learned are not adequate to make me understand the meaning of life and the purpose of our being. Let it be said that he did not know the meaning of life from early childhood on and never came to see that life has to be lived to the fullest. Instead I wasted away the time with all kinds of trivialities. Yes I wrote some books and did try to explain myself as it were but to what purpose. It seems to me that the expression No man is an island is totally false, at least not true in every case. I seem to prattle on and on but the real meaning of what I want to say becomes lost somehow as if it wants to escape my thought process. I would like to follow the well-defined lines drawn in the sands of time that make a person or a nation great but every time I look upon these lines I realize that they are all of a temporary nature as they are overthrown in a matter of a few years when another set of rules appears that is more in tune with the times. The rules of permissiveness have become the norm and before one knows it all the old values by which our forefathers abided by are gone out the window and the new norm takes a hold to the detriment of many a nation. We don't have to go far back in time to see what a new way of life can bring a nation to. Germany being one of them: a nation that brought forth such great men and women and was the beginning of the great reformation of the Christian beliefs. How low did this once mighty nation fall under an absolute ruler named Hitler and his henchmen. And so it can be for an individual who strays from the straight and narrow, as the saying goes. Now I am here and I look back at my past footsteps and see the waves of time take them away forever.

AN INWARD JOURNEY

Going on an inward journey is not the easiest thing to do as it is almost a confession of the inner self. When I look back on my life and see all the broken promises and the wayward way of it I come to realize that so many people are so much better in their behaviour, one could say that the whole world is. Am I a coward, in a lot of ways I am because I shrink from responsibility and rather see others do the labour that makes this a better world. I have been called several names that are not complimentary and have shrugged them off as just a malicious way of getting back at me for the things that I have done perhaps unknowingly. I come across as a religious person but am I, or is it all a charade to make people see what I am not. It is a hiding out in the darkness as it were so I come only into the light when absolutely necessary and than not showing my true face. My thoughts are at times so terrible that I am praying that they will be taken away from me but I don't seem to be able to stop them. As the Germans say Die gedanken sind frei and no amount of willpower can prevent them from appearing whenever the occasion arises. Abusive they are as well as of a sexual nature at times and when I try to stop them they seem to overpower me and the willpower comes to naught. Often I wonder if I am the only one that has these experiences or is everybody overcome by them, from that old lady down the street to the young men next door. And so I am coming full circle and back to where I started from the inner self that is at times in turmoil because of it. I was listening to the songs "My Country" and "Jerusalem" and I felt awe for those who have fallen in so many wars giving their lives for king and country. And then the question arises Would I give my life for my country or would I run and hide when the time comes. I realize that we all will die one day and if that day comes when we are unrepentantly confronted by that fact, will we be strong and take on the great reaper, with a sword in our hands, to slay the one who is always around when someone passes away. Will there be a longing in me to see the "other side" of which so many songs are written and of which so many sermons are spoken and books written, some soothing and others so harsh that speak of Hell and woes that will befall those who are not of the saved variety. I know it is so easily said and so many, especially of the academic world, cannot overcome their knowledge of the so- called real world and so cannot embrace the spiritual world. If you cannot see it, touch it, or comprehend it, it cannot be true therefore you discard it as fable. I have come to see that so many people perish unbelieving in anything, going agnostic to the grave, never knowing the way to salvation. I know that we are straying into the world of religion and perhaps it is just as well as that is the only reason that we are on this earth in my opinion. The way to receive salvation may not be the same for all religions. There are always a way to express one's self in one way or another as I am doing now at this very moment. The way to the all-knowing one is not an easy way and a lot of preparation must go before we are allowed into the presence of God Almighty. The cleansing of all wrongdoings committed during one's life must have taken place by lowering the whole body into a body of water and so be cleansed at least symbolically. I will stop here and hope to come back at a later date.

ON PATRIOTISM AND DIFFERENCE

I just finished watching the last night of the proms and was amazed at the love that the British people showed for their country and queen. It always amazes me how all this comes about. I have come to realize that from birth a child born is taught about their country, what it represents and what it stands for. In all the schools, children are educated and learn the history of their country, its achievements and its glorious past. They will sing patriotic songs to honour their country and are taught what it takes to maintain the status quo. They are taught about freedom and what is needed to maintain this freedom. In most countries an army is maintained to prevent it from being overrun by another nation. Sometimes the sacrifices made by the soldiers are of a dire nature as they lay down their lives for their country to prevent the enemy from taking away their freedom. So you see from an very early age it is instilled in the children and so also the grownups that at times sacrifices must be made. How dire were the consequences of the First World War and the Second World War. Could it all have been prevented or would all negotiations have had no effect on the Kaiser or on Hitler. I am sure that many debates continue to be conducted by those more in the know than I am and the results are probably like a futile attempt to put a broken egg back together. Anywhere on Earth where a head of state has it in his head to do something that would put him at the very top he has taken the opportunity regardless of the consequences. We can go to earlier times in history when Genghis Kahn, Attila the Hun, or Napoleon wanted to expand his empire to their own glory. I am sure that all these entities would not have listened to reason because there were always those who backed the plans made and were willing to bring them about and have their name included in what was going to be accomplished. When one comes to think of it, life seems such a fragile thing as pride and greed take over. When love is gone cruelty will take its place and no mercy will enter the minds of those who carry out the orders given to them by the generals in charge. The cruelties carried out even in today's world by those who have conquered other nations are still rampant. Most of them are done in the name of a religion or pure murderous hatred for fellow human beings of a different religion or race.

AND SO IT GOES

Needless to say a wish does not make it so. A person with no legs wanting to walk is not able to do so. The willingness is there but the ability is not. I look around some more and see people who are so much better than I am in ability and morally so strong that they could be compared to angels as it were. But I will not despair as the day will come that we all have one thing in common. We will have passed on and only our legacy, if you can call it that, will live on. For me it is in my children who have my genes and my blood in their veins that will be passed on to their children the same as it was passed on from my own father to me and from his father to him. So even though we are gone we will live on in our children and the next generations that follow. I know I may be rambling on and on when some of you read this but I am sincere in my thoughts and will write them down for whoever wants to read them. Perhaps you will find a comparison with your own life. We all are so unique and there is only one of us in this entire world. There may be lookalikes etc., but the being within is unique and there is no other exactly like us. The other day I was thinking about all the movie stars that I saw during my younger years and I wondered Where are they now. Is there a special place for movie stars in Heaven where they congregate and reminisce about the past or will we all be in a place were there is no distinction and we are all simply waiting for Judgment Day when we all will be judged according to our actions in life. When I watch an old movie as I have a tendency to do I am so sorry to know that even though they are alive on the screen they are long gone. I feel so sad and weep at times for them as they were such beautiful people and they seem to come alive again on the screen. If you came from an area where there were no movies available and had never heard of the movie stars you would think that they are alive indeed as they see them as they were and do not know that they are long gone. And so it goes. We have memories of the past and to most of us they are precious and not easily forgotten however whether a thousand years have passed or only a second it is all in the past and as it were it is all the same. A million years or the last second, it is all in the past and nothing can bring it back. When I look at the future I realize that I don't know anything about it and will not be able to change what will happen in the next second. Time is a strange thing as it holds us prisoner in its firm grip. Yes we will be able to change some things for ourselves, to go on a diet or stop smoking or have a baby, etc., but in the end it will be as it will be. I realize also that most of the great rulers of this world, whether it was Alexander the Great or the rulers of the Roman Empire or others who thought to bring something better to the world indeed did change the world as it was at that time but now that they are gone did it really make a difference? Life goes on whether you live in an oppressed state or a life of slavery or are free or ill or healthy or without a limb, on and on it goes and who is to say where it stops. This chapter seems to have no end and if there is one I will wait to see it and end it later on in my life. I don't seem to be able to.

ABOUT DEMONS

What can I say about demons as they seem to be everywhere including in me at times. There are forces in the world that are opposite like life opposed to death or good to evil or substance to antimatter. Demons have the ability to possess a being without it knowing that it is possessed. When we go back in history we see that the empires that followed one another were all led by people who were likely under the control of a demon or devil if you will. The likes of Attila the Hun or Alexander the Great the kings of Babylon or the rulers of the Medo-Persian Empire the German Kaiser or Hitler all were possessed with a demonic being and so doing its will as dictated. Where all this is leading us is a mystery to me but I can see that anyone committing an offense against another human being must fall into that category. We all live our lives as our parents or guardians taught us or try to anyway but sometimes we will open the door for the evil one to come in and to destroy our lives if we let it. Sometimes the willpower to reject this force is absent or is overcome and we end up in a tragic situation from which there is no escape. The very thought of disliking another human being can be the beginning of a murderous thought brought about by a demonic power. When I see people who possess powers that go beyond normal abilities you can be sure that a demonic force is at work. I have seen things done by a magician that defy logic. Perhaps a person may say What a pessimist, and they are probably right as I have a tendency to be like that, however anyone who has seen what I have seen has to admit that what they do is virtually impossible. Because of this I have come to see that in the end there is no time there is no present and no future it is all one. When we observe on the television or internet what the Hubble space telescope lets us see "We are but a speck of dust on a weighing scale" to quote David the King of Israel. Yet we won't affect the weight of what is being weighed in other words although we are more than the highest of mountains because we are alive, we still are very insignificant in the realm of the universe. Sometimes I think that all the world and all the people around me are there just for me and the illusion of that makes me feel like an important part of the universe while at the same time it leaves me feeling like a helpless individual who is tossed to and fro in the ocean of life.

WITH LOVE

Where has my heart wandered off to?
It has gone into this unknown world.
The sights I see are alien and strange.
I try to touch that unreachable but can't.

What is it that beckons me to go further?
To go deeper and deeper into that great abyss.
Where all thoughts are stored and where memories
from so long ago are buried and forgotten.

I shiver to think what I may dig up there.
Where is the part where love is stored?
Oh, there it is—it is a large box and when I
open it, it says "Love of self" and it startles me.

Am I like that? No really, it must be a mistake.
I loved a lot of people and now this?
Get me out of here and let me think about this
for a while, as surely I know what love is.

Or have I had it wrong all these many years?
Turning inward I experience a strange feeling
of inadequacy, of having been left behind
while others expressed their love so freely.

And I, holding back that essential part of life
that gives meaning to everything around me.
I see it now and as I stand back and look at myself,
I am suddenly overpowered by a force that opens

the eyes of my blind heart and now love rushes in
and goes into every crevasse of my being and I
become what others have always been—
alive again, forever more, with love to spare.

PERSONAL MEMORY

We will enter into the inner sanctum of a soul that has been around for nearly eighty years now. From early childhood until now, How did I arrive at this point of my life via all the broken ruins of the past. The memories of yore are still quite active in my mind; seem so far away and yet refreshed with time and perhaps are enhanced by events that somehow get attached over time. Time at times becomes a great deceiver and the accuracy somehow becomes tainted as it were as the past fades away in the distance. However the reality at the time was so firm that whatever we thought then remains anchored to the roots of our memory cells. We would like to have a clean path to where we were in the distant past and change some of the things we did, especially our indiscretions, but needless to say this is not possible unfortunately. I realize that we all struggle with some of the things we've done in the past and would rather forget that they ever took place but here we are and the baggage we carry stays forever with us. The passing of time as I already said seems to lessen as memories drift away and the past disappears in the distance, but sometimes an event in our lives brings it all back and we are at a starting point again and so it goes.

HOMEWARD BOUND

I am homeward bound my love don't leave me on the way
but stay with me until the end comes and my life is done. The
road I am on is not too hard but full of curves going off in
directions where no exits are and the end so dreary
that I don't want to wander off into a world that's alien to me.
I know with my broken wings I cannot go far,
I am a prisoner of my past from which there seems no escape
but I have to try and make it to where I am going just the
same so go on I must.

The sparrow still sings in yonder tree, so life goes on also
for me,
The ants are still busy building and caring for their offspring
and the bee is still visiting the flowers to maintain their
existence. The leaves are still green and don't know the fall
is on the way,
it will change them all a brilliant colour seen by all with an
eye for these changes and enjoys them.
As for me, what am I sulking about?
I am still able to see and hear the birds
and should not be so morose as there is still lots to do and the
soul is still within me and departure may be still years away.

When I look back on the road I once travelled and see all the
ruins of my life
I come to the conclusion that even though it is all a memory
the vision seems so real that I am scared all over again and

my life comes to a standstill once more and the overpowering
feelings come to the fore and leave me so sad,
but I must go on, with a strong heart and sober mind, and so
I will.

MY YOUTH

When I was young and looked at the world through the eyes of a youngster it looked like a big ball of candy and I could not get enough of the great taste of it.

When I was getting older I realized that all was not sugar and spice but that the world was a place where there was not always peace and quiet and that the people you knew were not always what they seemed to be.

My dear parents tried to prepare me for the world that was to come and gave me advice in a great number of things but I thought that I knew it all and was prone not to listen to them as I should have. As a teenager I was somewhat rebellious and would do things that were not on the up and up and did get in trouble with the law at times for my misbehaviour but was lucky to have an understanding judge who let me off with a warning.

As I got older and was getting an eye for the girls I became more mellow and sexual thoughts were never far away from my mind not realizing that this was only a byproduct of a true and lasting relationship. The temporary relationships with girls always ended and then the One came into my life. My love for her blossomed.

ANOTHER WAY TO
LOOK AT THINGS

While listening to Bach's "Jesu, Joy of Man's Desiring" and other masterpieces I felt so alone and almost helpless. I try to get into what the composer was thinking when he wrote them while admiring the ability to do so. But who am I and what are my accomplishments in this world. Yes I wrote a number of books and made a little dent in the world of authors but compared to so many others it is just a drop in the bucket. All the great composers of the past are not with us anymore but their music lives on through the people who can read their music and interpret their music. I often wonder Where are they now. Are they in a place unknown to us until we ourselves enter there after our demise. The spirit world seems so far away at this time but we all know that this can change at a moment's notice. So many people got up this morning not knowing that today will be their last thanks to an accident on the highway or a heart attack or any other mishap that could befall any one of us. It is not a happy thought I know but still I think it quite often as it seems to pop into my mind of its own volition. I have been writing these short thoughts on my computer so perhaps I can know myself better by reading them. Sometimes it's like I am standing from afar and seeing myself in a mirror, my good side don't look too bad but my bad side is in a sorry state and we will not linger there for the good of us all.

THIS IS ME

To say to oneself Woe is me is not easy especially when we know that one day it will be asked of us to give an account of ourselves and the life we have lived and even when I know it so well I am still not reconciled with God's forgiveness for me, even I sin every day more and more and the sins committed are piling up on my shoulders. Sins committed against my own family and also the people who have trusted me are endless. I have run out of excuses and can only blame myself. I am so afraid of the accusing fingers of so many people who in the hereafter will be there condemning me to Hell as that is where I belong because of the way I have lived my life, unthinking of others and saying things that are not to be said. Me who knows so much, or thinks he does, about religion and who has written several books about it will have no excuse when the day of reckoning comes. I am so ashamed and words fail me. To say I am sorry is just not enough even though I would lay down my life for anyone it would not be enough to undo the deeds committed and done to others especially my family. Oh the shame I feel seeing how everyone is a better person than I no matter who it is. Oh God I need so much forgiveness that only Christ the Saviour of all souls who will undo all misdoings and take upon Himself all our sins and cleanse us of all unrighteousness can absolve me. Oh Jesus where are you why do you hide your face from me. I am so lonely and so far from everything pertaining to Your word and deeds. Lord come to me in the night and open my blind eyes so that I may see as it must be seen before the great day comes that I will be no more and lay down my head to rise no more. It is like the apostle Paul said, I know about the things that I should do but for some reason I do the things that I should not do instead. Oh who can release me from the body of this death. Older and older we become and the visions of grandeur are slowly slipping away and the thought of everyday living is what remains, the fire is going out slowly but surely and we don't realize it until we stop for a minute and go back and think about this and then a burst of energy takes hold of us and we open our eyes to see where we have been and where we are going until the lapses come again. We are so weak and so brittle that even the slightest breeze slows us down. I realize that even as I write this it is not so for everyone. Some are active until their last breath, but this is me.

A SPECK OF DUST ON A WEIGHING SCALE

What is it that a prayer to God Almighty should contain and to whom do we send up this prayer. I as a person have nothing to offer Him who is the Creator of us all and the only thing he wants from us is that we will be worthy to enter into His house when the time of our passing comes. As for me I see myself as totally unworthy of this honour as my life has been a life of sinning and unbelief. Yes I know it so well and I have written about what is needed and have seen the total inability to please my Maker. I have come to see the miracle of the Christ figure and the need for Him to come into this world to save so many of us. The way He accomplished this was a life of torture as it were, seeing all the unbelief of the people in all the miracles he performed even when they witnessed them with their own eyes. As we read the story of Jesus in the Bible we see it all as handed down from the disciples to us. How dare we even speak to God in our lowly state. We are to him a speck of dust on a weighing scale, as David put it so precisely. Still the spirit within us is what it is all about, this spirit that cannot come into the presence of God because it is so contaminated by earthly behaviour. God requires from us a soul as it was at the beginning of time when we were all in the presence of God before we were even born. We had to go through this life to experience the same as Christ did and not be waylaid by the wiles of the ruler of this world and to be steadfast and to become as Christ and understand the meaning of it all so that we will be cleansed from all our sins and made worthy to enter into the Kingdom of Heaven.

MY SONG

My song, it is not beautiful but from the heart
I really don't know where to start.
My heart, it speaks to me with needs
For love and happiness in deeds.

Who is the one who understands
The longing for the reaching hands?
The need for sunshine in my life
From friend, my family, or wife?

Is there no ending to my sorrow?
Will there be for me tomorrow?
Why must I remain in want?
Why does no one understand?

Am I indeed an island now,
As I sit here with puckered brow?
I realize that it is mostly me
Who stands aside and lets them be.

NOTHINGNESS

The fist of anger raised will not be raised again.
The angry words once spoken will be heard no more.
The proud are now so lowly bound
when they are put into the ground;
The singing lark will now fall silent.
The ear that heard can hear no more.
And blind the eye that saw so much;
there will be all encompassing silence
as all who were will be no more.

No more, no more, no more, no more
Because we'll sleep forever more.

THIS AND THAT

Whom have I here on this earth. Are there any who really know me. God knows my heart and I long to be within the gates of the heavenly Jerusalem where I will be safe and nothing can touch me or scare me. The loads of sin and my earthly baggage will all be gone and only my voice will be heard to sing praises to him who died for me in my stead. I can bring nothing with me and anything that I have done for the good of mankind or my fellow human beings is nothing compared to the sacrifice made by Him who laid down His life so that we may live forever. How great this is will only be seen and known when we are there in this safe haven. The seeing of God's anointed will be too great for us to understand and will leave us speechless at the first but then, together with all the other souls, we in unison will praise His name, Emanuel forever. I feel my life is slipping away from me and my time is close at hand. Why I feel this way I cannot tell you, but perhaps it is a second sight. May the Lord have mercy on me, a terrible sinner who does not even deserve to undo the latchet of His shoe.

YOUNG MINDS TODAY

That I have wrestled with this question is putting it mildly. Jesus said that Satan did not want to have anything to do with Him as He was the enemy of Satan and his cohorts. I have come to see that in everything we see and hear Satanic forces are at work. Most of us enjoy one game or another to pass the time here on Earth, whether it is on TV or the living room table in the form of a board game or a card game of sorts. It is all to take us away from the road to salvation. When we count the many hours spent on entertainment we must admit that they count for probably half a lifetime. We seem to have a need to be entertained as we become too bored with life itself and so go out to watch a movie or to see a play that is then forever with us. I am the greatest user, I know as I am bored easily and turn to one form of entertainment or another. I see it in myself and still the self-discipline is not there and I seem to get overwhelmed as it were to do what comes into my mind. The words that Jesus spoke when he said "Pray without stopping" echo in my mind and soul and still I wander into that minefield that is Satan's world and become ensnared by that evil entity over and over again. And I want to say with Paul, "Oh, who shall free me of this body of this death." Where the solution lies is not for me to say other than that we must escape as it were from the prison that is our own self, where all the thoughts are formed, and pray to God Almighty that we may be spared from the clutches of Satan as that entity is very powerful.

The story of Job in the Bible is enough to realize that he is the ruler of this world and only the very strong with God's help can escape his clutches. In today's world when the internet can be used for good as well as evil it is very easy to come across things on there that are not to enrich our knowledge for our own good. It is a pool of dirt where the most vile things are exposed especially to the young minds who are so impressionable. The handheld games seem to get the upper hand of most youths and the parents are at their wits' end as to how to stop the onslaught of Satan upon their children. We are seeing a falling away of whatever was valuable in our days to a devil-may-care attitude and our children seem to run to a gaping abyss from which there is no escape like the lemmings do when the population is getting too large to sustain them. The violent games on cell phones have become an obsession, and to act out whatever is shown has now become a trend. We only have to read the newspaper to know that this is true and young people don't hold life sacred as they once did.

The "better than you" attitude is coming to the foreground more and more and we can see it in any game that exists in this world whether it is a mind game or a physical game it does not matter. So what are we to do about all this I ask myself and the answer escapes me every time. I have come to realize that weapons of any kind are readily available to many a young person and shootings and stabbings are an everyday occurrence. Young lives seem to be worth a dime a dozen and the influences that play themselves out on these young people are such that only the strongest are not influenced by them and the reason for this in my opinion is because of their upbringing by responsible parents. A lot of parents think that the toddler will raise him or herself and don't seem to see that a certain amount of discipline is needed to keep the youngster from growing up wild without the knowledge of right and wrong. So often I see children telling their parents what they want instead of the other way around, they become in charge and if not challenged and put straight will become a lost generation. In today's world the availability of drugs is a curse to our youth especially those who are so easily influenced to try this or that whether cannabis or pill or powder and then because of that become dependent and a vicious cycle is started. Many a young life is ruined and many a fine start ends up in misery to the sorrow of parents who had the best intentions but failed to make their children aware of all the dangers that are out there. Well I had my say and even this does not make things all right for it is only a warning as to what could happen to a child if they are not made aware of all the dangers out in a world of fun and games.

PAST SENSE

When I look back on the times gone by
And feel the emotions again of the past
I wonder whatever possessed me to wander
Down the path that led me to this sorry state.

I know that to see me you hardly do notice
The aches that so torment my heart for so long
But go on I must as time does some healing
Although ever so slowly, as memories last.

Who knows what the future will bring to us all
The hopes and the fears of whatever befalls us
What is it that plays on our mind and our soul
To keep us going in this circle again and again.

I know they all say, don't live in the past
Look forward and enter a new way of life
That will make you happy and not sad
It is easy to say for those not in my shoes.

At ease with myself I must become
On the gentle waves of my thoughts
The blue skies that hover over my soul
Try to dispel the gathering clouds of fear.

Religion creeps in and gives me thoughts to wonder
What path to take, instead of lying down in slumber
Wake up I must as time goes by so speedily
Get hold of the truth, which always sets one free.

I wrote this down to speak to myself and wonder
What is inside of me and to impart to others
That no one is alone and no one is an island
No matter what, it's only love that can cure all.

PEARLS OF WISDOM

A day without sunshine is a nice day too
The hearing of laughter can be a curse to some
An inquiring mind is an opening flower
In a child we see eternity
A dog's wagging tail shows pleasure
What good is a ship without a rudder
A small act may lead to big things
Easy to please is an excellent trait
A cause can convert millions
Rapture is outrageous laughter
Freedom is normal for those who don't see
To take and not return gives off a foul odour
A blowhard has no wind
A narrow mind has on blinkers
The straight and narrow road is full of curves
To belong is a great gift
Time will cover all wrongdoings
The universe is full of droplets depending on one's size
The weak may be stronger than they think
Rubber stretches only so far
A lark not heard still sings
A blessing can be a curse
A new dawn brings endless complications
Hope is an unseen thing
Good is the absence of evil
Even the strong have weak spots
All oceans consist of droplets
Mountains disappear one grain at a time

Some hours are long and some are short
One second can be a lifetime
A giant can be small in one's eyes
Envy is Satan's helper
Growth is that which comes naturally
Debris is building blocks
Beyond is out of reach

The dead are alive in our hearts
To the thirsty, one drop of water is worse than no drink
The good old days are now but we just don't see it
An erupting volcano is the earth's own anger
Fire cleanses all things
Realism is harsh reality
A Christian foregoes all rights
A double mind is like a candle in the draft
Progress is a step away from inertness
A title does not make the man
The morning has a mouthful of gold.

TIMELINE WALKER

As I walk on the beach of my hometown, at the water's edge, I look back and see my footprints in the sand. It's like looking into the past as I see my trail fading in the distance. The thoughts I had then have already been forgotten. I follow my trail to where I am now and seem to go from the past back into the present. I can hear the waves softly lapping against the shore and the seagulls are flying high, aloft, soaring, on the gentle breeze. Their cries may be directed at me for coming into their world or maybe just at each other, I don't know. In the distance I can see a ship slowly passing along the horizon. It seems to be standing still but of course it isn't. My shoes are crunching the seashells that mottle the beach, but my eyes are not on them as I do not care. My eyes are not on them but on the surroundings I am in on this early morning. There is no one around and the serenity revives my soul and all unpleasantness falls away as my eyes take in the vast expanse of sky. I try to become one with it all, to also float away upon this gentle breeze, to be carried to places as yet unseen. Try as I might I am earthbound and I pity myself. As I am getting close to the ramp where people come on the beach I see some coming now. For a moment I feel this beach to be mine and these people are intruding on it. I hate to share this moment, but they have just as much right as I have to be here. I turn around and start retracing my steps and with them I disappear into the past to get back to the present.

THE SEA OF MANKIND

When I look at the sea of mankind I see what has become of the old ways, the gentleness and the way people conversed with one another is now totally alien to today's youth. I realize that with the modernization of everything, the old ways have faded away and the new era of What can you do for me today has arrived, bringing with it problems that did not exist not so long ago. Quite a few parents seem to be at a loss as to what to do with their children because of the demands uttered by them. The world seems to be getting smaller via the airwaves, an event happening at one end of the world is being broadcasted within seconds to all who are interested. We see whole populations being expatriated from their homelands because of religious terrorist groups who want to force their will on the masses at gunpoint. There is no doubt that any time now there will come a breaking point that will plunge our world into chaos from which very few will escape. All the existing nations will be involved and the use of weaponry thus far never used will, to a great extent, make this world almost inhabitable. There is no escape, as you are either for or against and that will be the way of it, not only for the nations but also for the individual living on the land. The fear of the unknown will be ever before us and the dread of it all will make life miserable, especially for those with children. The war that will shortly come to pass will affect us all and to have a safe heaven is of the utmost importance to many of us. To write about all this gives me no pleasure but for some reason I have to. It is almost like an urge that lives within me and needs to be expressed or die within me.

HERE AND NOW

Here I am in this place and at this time reminiscing about the past and yet I don't seem to get any further than the present. I know my past is not as glorious as some people's but then I have lived a fairly sheltered life. No studying for certain goals or doing well in sports no vacations to speak of as the family could not afford them but nevertheless here we are all in one piece and breathing air. So now what, Shall I go on or shall I stop here. The world is so full of people that are far more interesting than I am and the stories they have are titillating and I sometimes wish I was more like them however I am what I am even if the stories I have are a bit on the boring side for most people. The most interesting thing about me is that I seem to understand the Bible having been brought up in a religious family where my father was the boss and we had to do what he told us to do. But that too is now past and we are free so to speak to do as adults what we like to do. I have come to realize that to become an adult brings so many responsibilities with it that it at times overwhelms me. The choices one makes in the course of a day, a month, or a year can affect the rest of one's life, like the road not taken etc. I often think about what is good and what is evil. It is easy to understand good but what is really evil. When I see what is happening in the animal world how predators kill and eat other animals then I see the similarities between good and evil. When we see the atrocities committed by so many people in the name of a king, a kaiser or an emperor, then our hearts go out and our minds say, Why did this all happen. When we see the millions upon millions of young men going into battle to expand or maintain an empire and die for that cause, then I wonder what has changed, since all the so-called empires came to naught and very few are remembered except in the history books. At this very moment the ISIS movement is causing havoc with entire populations, causing them to flee, causing tremendous hardships not only for the refugees escaping but also on the governments that are now being overwhelmed by hundreds of thousands of displaced persons. It is said that when a poisonous snake is found, to safeguard oneself you must cut off the head of the snake. There is in the Middle East a war going on that nobody wants and the consequences of doing nothing about it is leading to a chaos that is equal to the Second World War when so many people were on the move to escape the enemy. The League of Nations that came about so many years ago and the United Nations and all the other organizations seem to stand on the side and let all this happen. The makers of weaponry are making a mint out of all this turmoil and don't really care who purchases their weapons as long as money is made. There is no solution, they say, but there is if only the powers that be stepped in and put an end to all these wars and the greed of the ones in power. I know it took more than five years to defeat Hitler and his cohorts but I am sure that if actions were taken against those who are the cause of so much chaos and mayhem it would end all the oppressions against mankind. Let Christian and Jew, Buddhist and Muslim live side by side in harmony.

ALIVE

When I look up into the sky
And see the Milky Way
I do often wonder why
And don't know what to say
I feel so little and so small
But never feel forlorn
'Cause I am greater than it all
I live and I was born
The universe is dead to me
Though beauty shows at night
No star will ever like me be
Alive when this I write.

THE SLAYER OF MAN
AND THE SON OF GOD

Let there be no doubt that the slayer of man is Satan and his cohorts. He was created from the beginning as were the angels when time as we know it now began. He was the leader of music in Heaven and had control over many things so that he thought he was as a god himself and actually challenged God for supremacy. God could not allow this and banished him from the heavens along with one third of all the angels that were in Heaven and who followed him rather than their Creator. God's plan has thus begun to replace the fallen angels with a new creation, namely the Earth and all the universe and the new human race from which would be chosen those of pure heart with an inborn ability to communicate with their Creator. I know it is a long story but we all know what the Bible teaches us about this. We as human beings can never replace angels unless someone, namely God's son, became the door to heaven so to speak. His atoning work purifies us from all our wrongdoing and sins committed on this earth. We are indeed not worthy to undo the latchet of His shoes, but nevertheless He made us worthy by His dying on the cross for our sins as there was no other way for us to keep access to the Father and Heaven.

THE STRUGGLES

What is it that brings this world of ours to the state it is in at this time. There are so many struggles in the field of manufacturing it is the struggle to produce the best product possible, to be on top and outdo other firms or factories. In government it is the struggle to become the one in power or control of the country, telling the people that this or that party has the answers to all our troubles. In the field of sports it is the struggles to become the best, to beat the other team for that trophy that will the reward the best team. Then there is the struggle to survive one more day in a world of poverty and sickness. The struggles of a government to impose a certain way of living upon its population in the form of a regime. The struggles in the Middle East to maintain a government that is being attacked by forces meaning to impose religious rules and regulations. When we think back to the past we see the many civil wars that have taken place in so many countries, how thousands upon thousands died for a dictator, a tsar, or another person who thought he was a better man to take over the reins of government. I often wonder about the manufacturers of weaponry. Weapons that are more efficient in killing a larger number of the enemy or citizens that are in the way of "progress." We went through two world wars and the number of people killed and maimed is innumerable and the memorials for them are proof of the sacrifices made by the soldiers who fought in them as well as the conflicts which came after those wars. When are we saying to those who produce arms and ammunitions enough is enough and make all the governments in the world say the same thing. I realize that so many people would be without a job because of it but at least the killings would stop after the bullets, grenades, and shells stopped coming. I know it is a very naïve way of looking at this but what else can we do to stop the exterminations of whole peoples. I fear that only when our time runs out will we have real peace.

54

THE FATE OF THE WORLD

As I sit here and contemplate life I come to realize how little we can hold or encompass. The eye can only see so far and the ear can hear only the things within range and just the same we think we are somebody. The world flies through space at tremendous speed and the surface of the earth itself has a speed of over one thousand miles per hour and here we stand thinking we are somebody. The atrocities committed in the name of a king or a ruler of a nation, tribe, or family are beyond understanding and seem to be rooted in a belief that as long as we ourselves are in safety it is all all right. What foolishness to think that we are somebody special. The empires of the past have all gone by the wayside though there may be remains of their existence. Nevertheless they are gone and all their sacrifices in the form of young men who fought for this or that ruler have been, in hindsight, in vain. Even now the world is full of people who have in mind to form a religious empire to whom all the world must adhere or be put to death. All the lessons from the past don't mean anything only the present is catered to. Is there a solution to this problem I wonder. As a boy I saw people of the Jewish faith being taken from their homes and put into trucks and taken to concentration camps. to be in the end be exterminated. There is no end to the cruelties committed by nations in power over the past two thousand years. One does not have to go very far back to when the atomic bomb was used during the Second World War to expedite its end. How tens of thousands were killed in a few seconds and thousands more died of the injuries. I believe us to be on the very edge of a war of a proportion that we have never seen before in which millions will die because of weaponry that will wipe out whole populations in a matter of minutes. There is no doubt in my mind that there will be atomic warfare as we have never seen it before and this will be the end of an age and the beginning of another, perhaps the age of Aquarius.

ELOHIM

Why these questions arise in me I don't really know, it seems that most people have the answers except me. I was thinking about who and what God is and what He is all about. I know one thing, that the Godhead is not just one but three in one called the Elohim and there is no separation at any time. These three created time in order to have everything we see come into being. Anything from the smallest atom to the greatest star or heavenly body in the universe. Seeing it all should make us stand in awe when we look at our own self and our so-called abilities. God is not some old man with a beard neither is the Son or the Holy Spirit they are as they always were. When God said let us make man in our image, the us was the Elohim. They made them in their strength and not as babies. That Adam had a full grown beard when he was created I very much doubt, I have no doubt that Adam being a male grew a beard later as razors were not invented at that time. We tend to see in paintings most of the older wise men with beards including Jesus, portrayed as a beautiful being, but they have not read Isaiah 53 were He is described as being rather poorly in health as well as appearance, so much so that we would not have desired Him etc. All we see was created by the Son on the command of the Father and is sustained by the Holy Spirit who instilled into everything the laws that govern it all. We may call this the laws of nature, what holds the tiny atom together to the laws of gravity and all the other forces that hold the universe in place. Anything that has life is also governed by the laws instilled within it. We don't have to go far to see this in everything from the smallest of plants to the greatest of animals. These laws also govern us all and the functions of our bodies testify to this. The only part of us that is separate is our spirit, or soul if you will, it is subject to other forces that cannot be explained except to say that evil forces can influence us to the extent that we will become a slave of whatever this evil force has intended for us to do. It is here that a belief in an Almighty entity is the only thing that prevents us from becoming a slave of the evil one. We must have an understanding of our eternal nature which is that part of us that gives us the desire to become one again with the Elohim, where we were when the worlds were formed, our soul was there and there must be in us a longing to become one again with the Elohim. The journey after birth on this earth is like a battleground because of the so-called free will given us at the fall of Adam and Eve. We have so many desires in us to please this earthly body that we tend to forget the need of our spiritual being to be immortal in that part that we were in before we were born. Let us look at nature and see how everything is regulated by forces unknown to us, from plants to animals to planets and stars and the universe yet to be discovered. We see that to everything there is an end and that nothing lasts forever except the Elohim.

HOW RELIGION CAME
INTO THE WORLD

The question as to why we need religion has been on many a person's mind. From this stems all the controversies as to the why's and why nots. We all have an idea and mine is that if there is a God there must be a way to contact Him, so when we embrace a religion we have perhaps found a way of doing this. As to where religion comes from, we have to go back in time as far back as creation. There are but few people who have not heard the story of Adam and Eve and of their relationship with their maker (God). All the religions in the world have one thing in common, namely a god or deity, or many, as its head. With it comes the practice of worship via the different rites and ceremonies. The Christian faith has the same origin namely through Adam his son Abel, who no doubt had offspring before he was slain by Cain, and so on we go to Enoch, to Noah, to Abraham, to the Israelites and from there to Rome and on to the reformation until we come to the King James version of the Bible that has in my opinion the best translation from the Greek and other languages like Hebrew etc. I have come to see that religion is a very personal thing and brings with it a belief in the things unseen. It is a total spiritual experience. There has to be an understanding that there is an end to all things including our lives and then what. We have to see that the promise of eternal life is not an idle one. The Bible is a teaching tool that is given to us by God and He demands that we read it in order to gain an understanding of the workings of God in us through the Holy

Spirit and through Christ who is the door through whom we may enter into that realm where all things are clear and are given an assurance of eternal life with no strings attached. I see that some words are more powerful than others as in all subjects and I see how wonderful it is to be able to read and understand the meanings of whatever is written. Some people have the ability to say things so eloquently and we have to admire them for that as it too is a gift. I too in my own humble way try to convey to the readers of this chapter how religion came into the world.

WHO, WHAT, AND WHERE

Who am I and what is my purpose in this life that I have. Is it only to be born and to go through my young years and graduate to a teenager and then an adult. Now that I am a grownup, what is it that I am or have become. Are all the experiences learned by now able to make me a responsible adult? Life seems to have taken a step in a direction that we cannot stop as life goes on and whatever is coming our way we have to accept. A young man or woman comes into our life and it seems to change everything. The hormones act up and we believe ourselves in love and before we know it we are married and the children are on the way. I know I am going too fast, trying to get to the point that I am making, which is our eternal soul that is an attachment of us and we cannot get away from like it or lump it. So what about this soul? There are many books written on this subject and there are religions that have from the beginning of time expounded on this part of our being. Whatever your religion, the books on this are in plentiful supply. It is of a truth that there are what we call "bad" people in this world of ours and there are "good" people. Often I have wondered whether there are "neutrals" who are neither "good" nor "bad" but live among us. When I look inward I have to admit that I am one of them who takes things as they come. I guess in a way I am dead to the world even though there is a flickering of interest in the world's affairs and in the news on television. I am mostly looking for something that is really of value but most of it is about violence and mayhem. There are too many people who think they will never die and do want they want to do, to them it is all about the here and now and never mind the rest or eternal life for that matter. The atrocities committed by these people in power are of an unspeakable nature and to think that I too am a part of this human kind that in reality is inhuman. What I am trying to say is that the difference between them and me is very minimal although it does not seem to be so. When I think about all this I am so sorry for these people who commit these atrocities as they have lost all feelings and the word love does not ever enter their minds nor compassion. I am thinking about the people who are in the employ of a state or country who have to fulfill a role in society like the executioner who pulls the electric switch. What are they feeling when the event occurs. I don't know. I was just thinking out loud for a moment. There is no end to it all and suicide bombs are the new way of doing away with a lot of innocent people for whatever purpose, religion, power, disruption, or just the thrill, if you can say that, to commit murder and the promise of an afterlife that is out of this world. We are standing on the sidelines seeing all this happening and there is not a thing we can do about it except report what we see and experience. Anyone who believes that there are good and evil forces in the world or residing in mankind will come to the conclusion that it cannot go on and on and that a great cleansing as it were has to take place. But how this will come about. Very few people know although it is generally believed that this will happen through divine intervention. At this time we can go on the internet and find a lot of people who seem to have the answer and give warnings of a global catastrophe in the making which will occur in the not-too-distant future. To read or not to read, that is a question for all those that look at this book and hopefully see in this book the things I have seen. I went through the Second World War as a child and saw many things that a child should not see or experience and it did something to my way of thinking although it taught me also valuable lessons for my future as an adult.

ABOUT THE AUTHOR

I guess some may want to know if i have written any other books and I have indeed written 5 books one is call *"Poems and Stories for Children"* and one called *"Poems from the Heart"* and *"Religious Thoughts Stories and Poetry"* as well as *"Poems and Stories from a Prisoner's Troubled Heart"*. You can find my books on Amazon books or Barnes and Noble. I love playing games and enjoy a game of checkers and chess as well as card games of any kind. I have been a sailor for a while and was in the army for two years. I went through the second world war as a child of five to ten and had some scary experiences through that time that have stayed with me to this day.

www.ingramcontent.com/pod-product-compliance
Lightning Source LLC
Chambersburg PA
CBHW022101150726
47990CB00003B/1188